I Love Cats

Sue Stainton Anne Mortimer

Katherine Tegen Books
An Imprint of HarperCollins*Publishers*

HarperCollins® and ☕ are trademarks of HarperCollins Publishers.
Text copyright © 2007 by Sue Stainton
Illustrations copyright © 2007 by Anne Mortimer
Manufactured in China.

Library of Congress Cataloging-in-Publication Data
    Stainton, Sue.
    I love cats / written by Sue Stainton ; illustrated by Anne Mortimer.
        p.   cm.
    Summary: A celebration of the many kinds of cats and the various things they do.
    ISBN-10: 0-06-085154-6 — ISBN-10: 0-06-085156-2 (lib. bdg.)
    ISBN-13: 978-0-06-085154-5 — ISBN-13: 978-0-06-085156-9 (lib. bdg.)
    [1. Cats—Fiction.] I. Mortimer, Anne, ill. II. Title.   PZ7.S782555Ial 2007
[E]—dc22   2005018100

1 2 3 4 5 6 7 8 9 10   www.harpercollinschildrens.com

To Mum and Dad
—S.S.

For Polly, Annie, Ester, and Flora
—A.M.

Cats, cats, cats.
I love cats!

BIG
CATS,

little cats.

Thin cats,

fat cats.

Hairy cats, scaredy cats.

Angry cats,

cool cats.

Spotty cats, stripy cats.

Purry cats,

whirly cats.

Cats on your head.

Cats in bed.
I love cats!

Cats, cats, cats.
I love cats!

Giggly
cats,

wiggly cats.

Flying cats,

trying cats.

Dancing cats,

prancing cats.

Wiry cats, fiery cats.

Singing cats,

swinging cats.

Cats that wink, cats that think.

I love cats!

Cats, cats, cats.
I love cats!

BUBBLY
CATS,

snuggly cats.

Hoppy cats,

floppy cats.

Bumbling cats, tumbling cats.

WEIRDY CATS.

beardy cats.

Cats in your pocket,
cats in the drawer.

Cats in the kitchen,
cats in the hall.

Cats, cats, cats.
I love cats!